The Animals of Plashes Wood
Spiney the Hedgehog
written and illustrated by Graeme Sims

FREDERICK WARNE

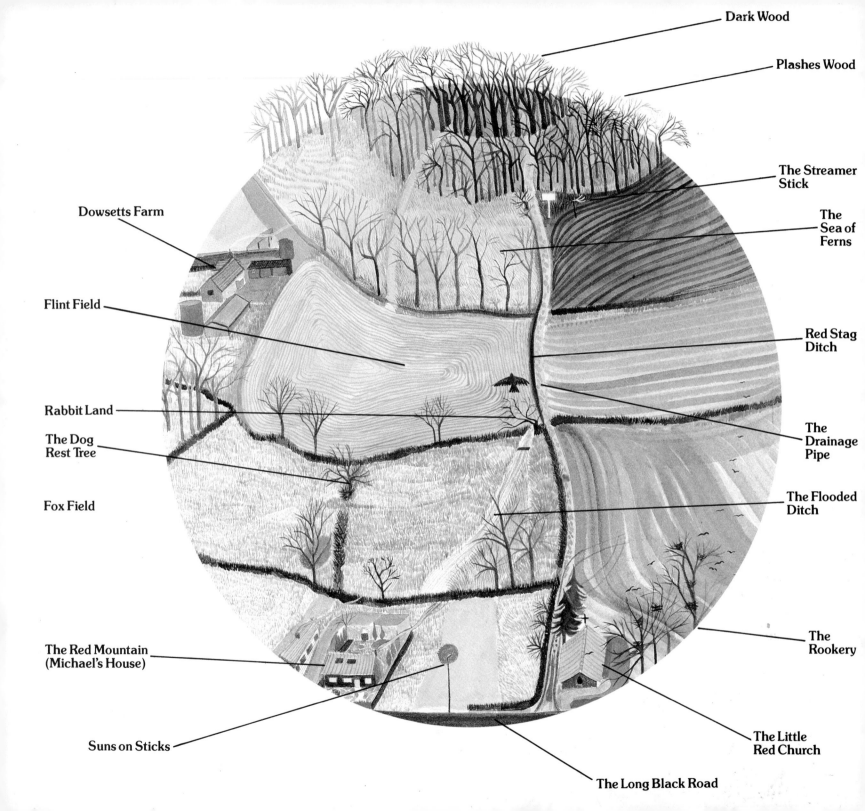

Dark Wood

Plashes Wood

The Streamer Stick

The Sea of Ferns

Dowsetts Farm

Flint Field

Red Stag Ditch

Rabbit Land

The Drainage Pipe

The Dog Rest Tree

Fox Field

The Flooded Ditch

The Red Mountain (Michael's House)

The Rookery

Suns on Sticks

The Little Red Church

The Long Black Road

I must confess that I have always been a bit jealous of Graeme Sims. Why? Because he is both a talented artist and a very good naturalist. Now he has added authorship to his list of attributes, and all I can say is 'Great! What a superb series of books!' Each one is a collage of accurate fact, recorded both in words and pictures — wholly believable fiction *and* an accurate knowledge of both the media in which he works and the countryside in which he and his creatures live.

Open the covers, and take a look at the landscapes, from hedgehog, mouse or rabbit level, snuffle through the leaves, poke your nose or paws into the cool dark soil, meet trees root first, wander amongst the bluebells (above and below), and learn about the countryside in which you, yes *you,* live.

Plashes Wood, Flint Field and Rabbit Land are real places. What is more they are not only just around the corner from the Sims house, they are not too far away from all our homes. Even if you live in the centre of a city you can find a Plashes Wood, waiting for you to discover, only a short bus ride away.

How lucky we are, for despite its size, its population and its history, Britain is still in essence a rural country, a diversity of landscapes created by man and yet still providing habitat for many of its natural animals and birds. Unfortunately, the path of change is today very rapid and one must ask, how much longer will this happy and beautiful state of affairs continue?

If enough people read these books, take note of what they say and learn to understand their own Plashes Wood as well as Graeme and Michael Sims know theirs, the answer is forever.

DAVID BELLAMY
Bedburn

Copyright© 1983 Graeme Sims
First published in Great Britain by Frederick Warne (Publishers) Ltd, London, 1983
Book Design by Sims-Lardeaux & Co, Hertford
ISBN 0 7232 2995 3

Phototypeset by Tradespools Ltd, Frome, Somerset
Printed in Great Britain by Wm Clowes (Beccles) Ltd.

The path from the village to Plashes Wood was churned up. It was worse where it wound narrowly past the little red church. The wheels of tractors and the feet of horses had made it wet and rutted. It stuck to my wellies like treacle until, instead of feet, I became the owner of large unmanageable blobs at the end of my legs, that sploshed and slipped on the ground.

Plashes Wood sits on the top of a hill and spills over the edges like custard on a Christmas pudding. It is surrounded by a rolling sea of fields, some littered with flints some at that time of the year just greening with the coming wheat.

The only sound was the March morning wind which hammered and battered at my ears and made cold tears run down my even colder cheeks. Even the long black road was silent.

I moved on into the woods, envying the sleeping villagers eiderdown warm in their beds, past the notice that warned of traps, and past a stick with a paper streamer that marked the path of the shoot.

Here in the wood the wind, broken by the black trunks, became a gentle breeze hardly rustling the deeply littered floor of leaves and bark and twigs, and rattling last year's empty acorn husks.

Snuffling and snorting through the sea of leaves and twigs came a hedgehog looking for an early breakfast of worms or frogs or mice . . .

Deeper and deeper into the wood went Spiney. It was cold here—dark and still. No creature stirred the leaves, no bird flew.

Spiney stopped, troubled by the silence. He looked around. Strung between the black-trunked trees was a bright orange baling twine and on it, hung by the necks, were rows of bodies, eyes still, teeth exposed—silhouettes ghostly quiet against the cold sky. Rats, weasels, grey squirrels, crows, gently swinging like washing on a line.

Spiney was used to death. In the world of the woods death was commonplace. Animals ate each other as a normal, and quite natural matter of course. But what kind of creature hung its victims in lines, uneaten, to swing silently in the trees?

Spiney moved on quickly and without his usual snuffling, putting as much distance between him and the lines of swinging bodies as he could.

Soon he was in the open, crossing the hillside and heading towards the fields surrounding the woods, paying no heed to the danger of Badger or Fox.

By now he was in Flint Field which runs uphill to the village. The going was heavy and Spiney, dodging the ever-growing puddles, and trying to avoid the jutting out flints, was becoming exhausted and also very hungry.

At the edge of a puddle two fat worms, probably believing it was April, had come up from their deep winter tunnels.

Spiney did not need a second chance—
he ate them both, snuffling with pure pleasure
over the mouth-watering meal. Things
weren't as bad as he thought they were.

Looking up from his breakfast he saw
four thin hairy trees rising from the mud.
They had not been there before, he was sure
of that. This was very unsettling. Trees surely
did not walk about!

From somewhere above the trees came
a snort and then the trees jumped. Spiney
was terrified. He quickly curled himself in a
ball and lay still.

Then there was another snort. Being curled in a ball is fine, thought Spiney, but if I stay I won't be able to see what sort of strange tree this is that jumps about and snorts. He unrolled himself, just enough to look up.

There, huge and dark stood Red Stag, the rain streaming off his thick coat.

'Never walk across the middle of a field!' said Red Stag. 'It's far too dangerous. Quickly! Come into the ditch where nobody can see us.' Red Stag bounded forward to the ditch and Spiney scurried along behind. In the shelter of the ditch, the rain and wind was less fierce.

Spiney explained to Red Stag why he was so far away from home, and related the horror he had seen in Dark Wood.

Red Stag listened carefully, nodding his head wisely as Spiney told his story.

Then he said, 'You're obviously a very young hedgehog and you won't become an old one unless you're very careful. Watch out for Fox,and Badger, but even more dangerous is Man.' With that he nervously looked around him, leapt out of the ditch and was gone, in a flurry of raindrops and flying mud.

Spiney was puzzled—he knew about Fox, although he had never met one, and he had heard about the terrible Badger. But Man—what was Man?

In the ditch it was still wet, but at least the rain and the wind did not batter him so much, and what is more there were worms everywhere. Before long Spiney's stomach was bulging with the worms he had eaten. He looked around for somewhere warm to sleep. Half-way up the side of the ditch was a drainage pipe. Inside it was warm quiet and dark . . .

When he awoke all was still. The rain had stopped and the wind had gone completely. He emerged from the pipe. It was night. The round moon lit up the countryside which now looked strange and dangerous.

Spiney was hungry again after his long sleep. He began to look for more worms, but the cold night frost had driven them deep down into their tunnels.

Spiney stopped stock still. Ahead of him in the light of the moon was the fattest mouse he had seen for a long, long time. It paid no attention to him. It seemed to be frozen—listening for something. Spiney dashed forward, eyes fixed on his quarry. Just as he was about to leap on it, something grey, soft and silent swept across his path with a whooshing of wind, and Mouse was gone.

Owl, the silent hunter, had heard Mouse, and had nearly put an end to Spiney as well.

Now Spiney was shaken. The woods were much safer than this terrible place where there was nowhere to hide. In front of him was a wide field surrounded by hedgerows, divided by a ditch that had become a pond with so much rain. The moon's reflection rippled in the water and lit up the whole area coldly, so that everything was clear and stark and eerie.

He didn't want to cross this place. It had a feeling of fear about it, but there was nowhere else to go. Gradually he inched out into the field, repeatedly sniffing the air for danger.

Then he heard a drumming noise. Something, or some things, were running straight towards him. Spiney was numb with fear. For a moment he could not roll up into a ball to protect himself. With an explosion of fur and feet, they hit him, bowling him over in somersaults towards the pond. They screamed in panic, 'Fox! Fox! Fox!'

'It's no good rolling yourself up into a ball, my little dish. Many hedgehogs have tried that trick before—and very tasty they were.' It was Fox! He dribbled as he thought to find some way of unrolling Spiney. If he could tempt him to swim then he could get at him from underneath.

'Your only chance, my little prickly dinner, is to jump into the pond and swim. We foxes cannot swim, you see,' said Fox, lying through his teeth.

Here is some good news, thought Spiney. I can swim like a fish! Here's my chance to escape. Then it dawned on him. How did Fox know hedgehogs could swim? He must have tried this trick before. Spiney rolled himself up tighter than ever. Fox nudged Spiney towards the pond. Spiney felt his hot breath, as nudge by nudge he was pushed closer to the water.

This is the end, thought Spiney. If I swim he will be able to eat me and if I don't I will drown. He waited for the next nudge that would send him toppling into the pond. Fox would be able to stand in the water with his long legs and finish off Spiney with ease. The next nudge never came. From far over the field came a bark. The farmer's dog was out. Now, the one creature that Fox feared and hated was the fierce dog that belonged to the farmer. The dog didn't like Fox much either. Fox placed his mouth next to Spiney's ear. 'There will be another time,' he said, and disappeared as instantly as he had come.

Spiney was stiff and very cold when at last he dared to unroll. He moved on, keeping close to the hedgerow, not noticing the little red church with a cross on the top as he passed by. Suddenly he came upon the most awful thing he had ever seen. It was long and black but lit to a bright and unnatural orange by lines of little suns on sticks. Even the sky looked bright and angry. Noisy monsters, fat ones with two lit up yellow eyes, thinner monsters with just one, dashed back and forth with a roar and a whoosh.

Hedgehogs seldom turn back, but this awesome place was too much for Spiney. He scuttled back into the protection of the hedgerow and made his way into open country again.

After a while he came to a black wooden cliff that went on for ever, or so it seemed to him as he walked along by its side—until he found a hole.

Spiney poked his head through the hole and sniffed the air. There were no enemies here. He felt safe. He pushed the rest of his body through, and made his way over the short, even grass until he came to a huge red mountain with holes in it, through which came bright lights and strange voices, the like of which he had never heard before.

There was a swishing sound and the light became very bright and Spiney could see inside one of the holes. Looking out was a creature. It stood up on its hind legs. It had a pink face with a pile of hair on top and seemed to be covered in strange stripy material. Spiney started to turn back.

The creature spoke in a language Spiney did not understand. 'Mum, Mum, there's a hedgehog in the garden.' Another larger creature joined the stripy one at the window and they both looked down at a rather startled Spiney.

'How lovely. Hedgehogs are wonderful for the garden—Dad will be pleased. I expect he is hungry. I'll make him some bread and milk.'

As Spiney tucked into the delicious bread and milk, he felt no fear. In fact when the animal called Dad arrived, his huge black feet smelling comfortingly of mud and leaf mould, Spiney felt very much at home. Fox, Badger and that dreadful creature Man would not catch him here . . .

'Can we keep him, Dad?' asked Michael.

'Only as long as he wants to stay,' I replied. 'He belongs to the wild, you know,' and I remembered the little hedgehog I had seen snuffling through a sea of leaves yesterday in Plashes Wood.